Elephant Bridge

Elephant Bridge

by Jeffrey Potter

Illustrated by Roberta Moynihan

New York
The Viking Press

For Job

Elephant Bridge

One

People say of Burma that it is a far country. And it is a country far across great oceans. But to the people who live there it is not a far country—it is their home. It is where all they know and love and hope is. Burma is their country, and they are called Burmese.

9

Even as here, there are children in Burma—and fathers, and mothers, and aunts and uncles; and toys; and dogs and cats, and birds and fish. And there are cities and villages, rivers and mountains and fields. And then there are jungles.

Much of the jungles is dark, and there are vines and creepers in them, and ferns and mosses, and flowers, and leaves so big you can hide in one. There are swamps too, and pools. And there are clearings where the sun strikes and it is light. Grasses sway in the wind, where on a hillside blowing they can look like flames leaping. It is these places that elephants like—especially at night, when there is no sun and the flies are still.

For there are elephants in Burma, and they look just as big to the Burmese as they do to us. Some are trained to work for man—pulling things, as horses do, lifting things with their trunks, like cranes, and pushing things with their heads, like bulldozers.

Others are not trained. They are wild elephants and live near the jungle and on the great plains, where they are safe from man.

Burma is a warm country, and part of the year there is nothing but rain. This is the monsoon season, when Burma is wet—and hot. The rest of the year there is no rain and Burma is dry—and hot. But the Burmese are used to this; they think it strange that in our country it is not the same. And they are glad it *does* rain, as we are, even though it comes all at once.

Our story takes place in the dry season during a time of war in Burma, when the enemy was fighting in the jungles, in the villages, and in the mountains, and the Burmese were afraid. For there were many of the enemy, and their guns were good.

And in the villages the young men were called by the army to go and fight. They were given what guns could be found, and bullets with them. And those for whom there were no guns took their *dahs*—short, wide-bladed swords—very good for cutting bamboo and sugar cane.

In a certain village of central Burma called Moying there was a boy whose name was Maung Po. And when Maung Po's brothers were lined up with the other young men by the village gate, ready to march to the war, Maung Po asked his father why he couldn't go to fight with his brothers. He said he knew he was small, but he was strong, and brave. Not as strong as his brothers, perhaps, but he was just as brave. He was certain of that.

Maung Po's father was the *Thugyi*—head man of the village—and ran all its affairs. And he smiled at Maung Po, whom he loved, and said he thought they could defeat the enemy without the boy's help. And Maung Po's brothers said sternly that war is men's work, and Maung Po but a child.

And the Thugyi laughed, for the brothers were barely men themselves. And all the people of the village laughed at Maung Po for wishing he was grown up and could go to war. For they knew that war is evil, and that in war

11

one must sometimes do things that are evil. And so they laughed.

Then the young men marched out through the gate, and the people of the village returned to their *bashas*—houses—in sadness. And Maung Po was left alone in the settling dust of the road, hating the people of the village for laughing at him. But he hated even more having to stay behind with the women and the old people and the children.

Maung Po thought much about this. He decided it wasn't because he wasn't big enough or old enough. It was because his father thought he wasn't brave enough—that was why he had to stay behind. If only his father understood that being brave had nothing to do with age or size, then he could go.

But perhaps others might know this, and instead of saying, "No, Maung Po—you cannot go!" they might say, "Yes, Maung Po—you can come!" And if he went to where the fighting was, they might say, "Stay, Maung Po—stay and help us fight!"

Once the war was over, he might even bring a medal home. And all the village would be in the road to welcome him. To welcome him—Maung Po—in his uniform and with his medal! It might even be a white uniform, and his medal would be big and of many colors, like the medal of his father's father in the glass case on the wall of his father's basha—the sun, the moon, and all the stars. And all in silver. And hanging from it a bright ribbon—

orange. And the writing on it would say, "For bravery."

Of course, Maung Po's grandfather hadn't come home with the medal—it had been sent. For he was killed in some war long since won, so he had missed the fun of being welcomed by all the village. But Maung Po intended to bring his medal home. He wasn't going to miss any fun!

And that night when all was quiet and the people of his basha were asleep, Maung Po set off for the war. He took with him some rice in water buffalo's milk in a covered bowl, and wrapped it in his best *longyi,* so it wouldn't be broken. A longyi? That's what Burmese men wear—it's like a skirt but can be tucked up around the thighs to make walking easier. And he took the small dah his father, the Thugyi, had given him on his last birthday.

As he went quietly in the moonlight past the sleeping bashas a dog barked; then, scenting Maung Po, was still. For all the animals of the village knew Maung Po, and they knew there was no harm in him.

The village gate gave a slight creak as he slipped it open just wide enough to slide through. And Maung Po thought it might be a long time before he heard the creak again. And he thought it must be a long trek to where the war was.

From the top of a near hill he looked back on his village. It shone in the moonlight, and he could see his father's basha. And he thought of his mother coming to his mat in the morning to wake him to go to the well for

water. But this morning there would be no Maung Po to send to the well. Let one of his sisters do it, thought Maung Po; for he was setting out on men's work.

Taking up his journey Maung Po knew his father, the Thugyi, would know where he had gone. And if he sent someone after him, it would take a brave man to march after Maung Po to war. And it would take a braver man to bring Maung Po home from the war.

Maung Po found the road to war a long one that night. He passed two villages, skirting round them through the rice paddies, so as not to wake the dogs, who might bark their alarm. And as the road wore on, leaving the rice country, it started climbing and became narrower. Trees crowded it close, and presently jungle began shutting out the light of the moon.

What a dark country this is, Maung Po thought, and sat down against a mossy tree trunk to rest. He laid his dah close to him and drank some of the milk of the water buffalo. Then, still holding the bowl, he closed his eyes and wished the road might be shorter, and easier, and show more of the moon's light. And he thought of his brothers and wondered if they had found the war. And he thought of his sisters and the well—his well. And almost, he wished himself back . . .

Feeling something wet on his arm, Maung Po, out of his sleep, thought, Now I have spilled the milk of the water buffalo and shall go hungry to the war. And then

he felt something warm and moist—it was snuffling at his arm—and suddenly he knew a feeling of danger. He lay there still, with his eyes shut, remembering the stockade with its gate that held his village safe—safe from *dakoits*—bandits—and safe from jungle life. And he thought of the stockade hard—so hard that he almost knew that when he opened his eyes he would see it.

And he opened his eyes, still not moving. It was just before first light, but already there was a slight grayness—just enough for Maung Po to see towering over him an enormous dark shape. And from the shape there hung a dark, weaving, vinelike something that gave an occasional little snort as it snuffled him.

Very slowly and carefully Maung Po slid his hand out along the ground for his dah. His fingers touched the hilt and he started to close them round it. Whatever this huge shape was, Maung Po knew one stroke might not banish it. And he also knew one stroke would be all he would have.

He edged the dah near to him, ready for the swing, and it clinked against a pebble. The great shape lunged at him, and he felt himself swept through the air, then held high, as if to be dashed to the ground. Almost in the same instant there was a single bellow and a heavy crash —and whatever was holding Maung Po fell. He was let loose and hit the ground hard, with the breath knocked out of him. He was again picked up by a vinelike something, but this time it seemed softer and gentler.

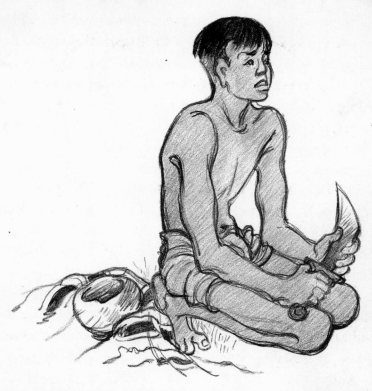

Leaves brushed against Maung Po, and he knew he was being carried along the road, held high. And all about him there was a strange shuffling noise, and heavy breathing. In fear he looked about him in the half-light and saw that he was in the midst of a herd of elephants raising a dust that choked him.

Gently though he was held in this elephant's trunk, Maung Po knew he could not escape. And he knew that even if he were set down, he could not stand, let alone run.

The herd, led by a giant bull elephant with tusks so long that they looked to Maung Po as though they could reach the top of the village gate, turned from the road and began following a jungle trail. It was much darker than on the road, and Maung Po wondered at how quietly the herd made their way along.

They followed this trail for what seemed to the boy a very long time. He got an occasional glimpse of the sun through the close-packed leaves of jungle growth and saw that it was high in the sky. And still the trek continued, and still in silence.

And Maung Po thought of his brothers and of the war he had set out for. And he thought of his village, bright in the warm sun; and of his mother, cooking rice for the noon meal; and of his sisters at the well; and of his father, the Thugyi—and he knew his father's sadness.

Maung Po was afraid. And he was tired, and hungry, and lonely. He didn't think of the medal for bravery now. He thought of his father's smile, his mother's voice, his sisters' laughter. And he heard in his mind the sound of the bucket falling deep in the village well.

Two

When they came to a clearing deep in the jungle the sunlight was so bright that at first Maung Po was blinded. Then, as his eyes became used to the light, he had a good look for the first time at the company he had been keeping.

They were elephants—no doubt about that! They were elephants, and there were more of them there than Maung Po had dreamed existed in all the world! There were great bull elephants, some of them old, with broken tusks and hides scarred from battles fought long since. There were younger bulls—warriors, Maung Po thought them—proud in their strength and courage. And there were cow elephants, looking to their young, their trunks ready with a swipe for any who might molest them.

23

As the herd gathered round a water hole in the center of the clearing, Maung Po noticed several bull elephants taking their places on the outer edge of the clearing, acting as guardians of the herd. They stood silently, facing the jungle about them and listening hard for any sound of movement. Maung Po squirmed in the grasp of the trunk slightly, to test its hold. It tightened hard for a moment, and then the boy was given a shake, as if by a cross and scolding mother.

He noticed that when the great bull elephant with the long tusks went to the water hole, the others drew back to let him drink alone. And drink he did, squirting water into his mouth with his great trunk and then squirting more over his shoulders so that it ran in streams down his back. He enjoyed himself thus for some time; then he suddenly stiffened, his trunk upraised as if he remembered something.

Slowly he made his way over to Maung Po, who felt himself being brought close to the ground, still held by the trunk. Looking up its length, he saw the massive head above him lowered, as though ready for trouble. And Maung Po saw that the rest of the herd were watching— watching and quietly waiting. Even the guardians turned their attention from the jungle.

Then the great bull was before him. Maung Po hadn't thought any animal could be that big. Close up, he was a lot bigger than Maung Po's captor, who till then had seemed as big as an animal could ever be. Slowly the bull's great trunk unwound and snuffled at him thoroughly, starting at his head and working along the full length of his body—pausing as if to consider, but still tense, as if not sure what it had found. Finally convinced, the elephant gave a sudden loud trumpet note. Maung Po felt the grasp of the trunk holding him relax and realized he had been laid gently on the ground.

The inspection was over. The great bull turned away. The rest of the herd lost interest in Maung Po too. Some returned to the water hole, while others grubbed about for bamboo shoots or special plants that might appeal to them. The guardians once more took up their watch.

As Maung Po lay there on the ground, too tired to get up, the elephant that had held him began nuzzling him with the tip of its trunk. It was very gentle and soothing. For a moment the elephant seemed interested in the tears that now covered his face; then it returned to its comforting. This was not the questioning snuffling Maung Po had felt before—it was more like a caress. Looking up at the head in wonder, the boy saw that there were no tusks and knew this must be a cow elephant.

Her eyes, so small for such a large head, surprised Maung Po almost more than anything else that had happened to him. His father had told Maung Po something of elephants, but he had never told him about the eyes—that they could seem so soft and warm, and carry such a sadness in them. They looked lonely, Maung Po thought —and here was a strange thing: an elephant lonely in the midst of a herd so large that there could be none in all of Burma that were not here.

Made shy of a sudden by something private seen in her eyes, Maung Po looked at the great feet spreading in and out as the weight they carried was shifted back and forth in a slow, rocking motion. It must be this spreading action that makes elephants so good in mud, Maung Po thought. For he had heard that elephants are better in mud than even the powerful tractors used in the south country, where the roads are hard, and the people of the cities go about in motorcars instead of bullock carts, like the people of his village.

Presently Maung Po's cow elephant wandered across the clearing and joined others, who were plucking leaves with their trunks from certain trees at the edge of the clearing. The boy noticed mothers giving their young bunches of leaves, and he saw one baby elephant who must have thought he wasn't getting his share butt at his mother's legs in anger. She gave him a swat with her trunk, but then soothed him with a particularly large cluster of leaves. The baby hadn't liked the whack much, and grunted, but the gift soon made everything all right. Maung Po laughed.

His cow elephant came back to him with a small bunch of leaves held in her trunk. She dropped them on the ground next to Maung Po and gave him a nudge. The nudge seemed more like an order than an invitation, and Maung Po stood up, again afraid. But the trunk picked up the leaves and held them out to him. He took one and with the sad eyes watching him, nibbled at it. He tried another; and it was sweet to him.

The trunk reached out for Maung Po's shoulder, then gently urged him toward the group of mothers. Then the elephant began pulling clumps of leaves from the highest branches, feeding some to herself and some to Maung Po. The more he ate of them, the better they tasted.

He was beginning really to enjoy himself when a couple of very young bulls ambled over to have a look at him. He drew back in fear, then felt himself picked up and placed atop the mother elephant's broad head, from where he could look down at the pair as from a tower. Their trunks reached for a little curious snuffling, but they soon lost interest and went to the water hole, where they began squirting each other. Maung Po wondered why he had been afraid.

/ A large fly settled behind the right ear of the great head under him, and Maung Po kicked at it with his heel to chase it away. The great body turned to the right, then waited. Maung Po looked up at the branch of the tree he had been fed from and shifted his weight toward it as he reached out. Too far. Annoyed, he gave a kick with his left heel, and the body slowly turned to the left. To his surprise, Maung Po found that when he gave a kick behind the right ear again, they turned to the right. Now really excited by his discovery, he gave a good kick with both heels, and the great hulk under him lumbered

27

forward. When he squeezed with his legs to get a firmer grip, the elephant stopped.

Maung Po laughed and, being thirsty, gave a smart kick in the direction of the water hole. And to the water he was carried. Once there, he leaned well forward and found himself lifted down to drink.

He drank deep, then bathed his hands and face. The water tasted a little muddy from the elephants' having stirred up the bottom, but still it was fresh. He felt the sad eyes watching him, and, turning toward them, he looked for a long time full in them. Maung Po smiled.

He wasn't surprised that soon they were joined by some of the young elephants. Under the watchful eye of his new-found mother they were polite. They all had to snuffle at him for a bit, then try encircling him with their trunks as if to try him for size. Finally one of them sucked up some water and playfully squirted it at him. *Whack!* went the mother elephant's trunk against the offender's bottom, and off they shuffled—looking, Maung Po thought, sorry about their bad manners.

Laughing, Maung Po followed them as they joined their mothers and soon found himself an object of great interest to the whole herd. There was what seemed an almost endless amount of snifflings, nudgings, rubbings, and encircling of trunks. When one of the babies playfully butted him, Maung Po went sailing through the air, to be caught by his mother elephant's trunk and swung up to her shoulders. In almost the same motion she

delivered a jolt with her shoulder to this newest offender that sent him sprawling.

Maung Po on his high perch was laughing so hard that his elephant had almost carried him beyond the clearing before he knew what was going on. He pressed hard with both heels to stop her, but this time it didn't work. Clearly she was off on a mission of her own, and this time without regard for any commands from him.

They entered a dark jungle trail, different from the one that had led them to the clearing; and from the way she settled down to a steady, shuffling pace, Maung Po sensed that this trek might be a long one. The trail had been little used, and the branches were so low that he had to lie flat along her head and hold hard to her ears to avoid being swept off. At times the trail was so faint that Maung Po wondered that she could follow it, but shuffling on she went, certain of her direction. As the jungle growth grew even thicker, she actually increased her speed.

It seemed strange to Maung Po that they should have left behind the friendly herd and struck off on their own like this. He wondered if the elephant might be after some particularly fine leaves or bamboo shoots with which to please him. Whatever might be the purpose of this trek, Maung Po knew that he trusted her and that in the end it would be good.

That she was not after delicacies for him he realized as they came to a sudden rise in the trail. Off to the left, where the afternoon sun filtered through the overhanging

vines, he could just make out under their layers of moss and creepers what he knew must be some strange, giant idols to unknown gods forgotten here in the jungle. He saw part of a stone staircase, with trees growing from its steps and walls so broken that only the vines covering them held them up. And as the mother elephant worked her way closer through the heavy growth he knew that he must be looking at a pagoda—or temple—so old that the gods must have died with those who worshiped them.

And then he saw, scattered round, great mounds of bones turned green by the steaming damp of the place. Some were so lush in growth of vines, it gave them the look of huge animals with leafy skins lost in the depths of their sleep. He almost expected to see the rise and fall of their sides with the breaths of their sleeping. And as his mother elephant picked her way among the mounds he knew he must be looking at the bones of whole herds of elephants who for centuries had picked this place to come to for their dying time.

Maung Po remembered having heard a band of ele-phant-hunters who had passed through his village on their way from the north country speak of elephants' dying places. These places all knew of, but none had found them.

And looking round him now at some of the great tusks sticking up through the vines, he knew why they searched. There was enough ivory here to buy all the rice paddies in Burma—and only he, Maung Po, knew. What a

32

secret to take home to his father, the Thugyi! With this much ivory his father could spend the rest of his days, not as thugyi of the village, but as thugyi of the whole valley!

Gradually Maung Po became aware of a stately swaying motion beneath him. It was almost a dance—a very slow and very sad dance. And he heard a soft moaning so filled with sorrow that he felt his tears close once again. But this time the tears were not for himself but were for the great beast under him that had cared for him so well.

Looking down, he saw the cause of her sorrow. For there at the base of a statue, and lying on a bed of bright jungle flowers, was a baby elephant, dead.

The boy slid to the ground and looked up at the mother elephant in wonder. Now at last he knew why he had been befriended, for he remembered the spilled bowl of milk of the water buffalo. And he remembered the elephant-hunters telling of how once they had trapped a cow elephant by first killing her calf. They had set out as bait milk of the water buffalo, and the cow had come to smell at it as she might her calf. And the hunters said they had almost caught a bull too, which had followed her.

And so Maung Po was sad and wished there were some way he might comfort her. He felt great love for her in her sorrow and wondered how he might show his love to so large an animal. He patted her trunk gently as it hung down limply and slightly swaying as she rocked from side to side. She was so sad she had forgotten all about him and knew only her grief.

Maung Po began thinking of his village and wondering how he would ever find it again, when, from behind, he heard a great crashing in the jungle. He turned to the mother elephant in fear and saw that she was so deep in sorrow that she heard nothing. He wheeled just in time to see the lead bull crashing out of the jungle. The bull gave one shrill trumpet of rage and was at her.

The impact was so great that Maung Po felt the ground beneath him shake. The mother elephant went down in a great fall, and, still enraged, the lead bull seized Maung Po and swung him high in violence, then hesitated. Gently he put Maung Po down and turned back the way he had come.

The mother elephant arose with a groan, picked up Maung Po, and followed with never a backward glance. Had the mother elephant been punished for mourning her calf, or was she punished for having shown Maung Po the dying place? Maung Po didn't know.

Surely the lead bull was an elephant of great importance, thought Maung Po, and so he should be called U Tun after U Tun Lwin, the rich man of the great belly and the many rubies who came each year all the way from Rangoon to buy the rice grown by the people of Maung Po's village. And he decided that he would call the mother elephant Ma Hla, for it sounded well when spoken. It sounded to Maung Po like what he felt for her—Ma Hla.

Three

It was dark when they rejoined the herd in the clearing. Maung Po, tired and hungry, was happy to have another meal of leaves. These had become scarce on the lower branches, however, so Ma Hla lifted him with her trunk, so he could reach higher than any of the young elephants. Maung Po felt their envy as he gobbled the choice leaves that were out of their reach.

The herd settled down for the night and formed a ring in the center of the clearing. Young ones and their mothers slept standing like horses inside the ring, while the bull elephants stood dozing on the outside with, as usual, three or four guardians posted at the edge of the clearing. Maung Po, still astride Ma Hla, slept with the best of them.

Much later, when all the jungle was still, one after another, the herd lay down and fell into a really deep sleep. Maung Po found that the most comfortable place to lie was on top of the great loose fold of Ma Hla's ear as it lay on the ground. It was soft and dry, and he could fold it over him as a blanket. As he was about to drop off again he heard a slight shuffling noise and looking up could see in the moonlight that the guardian bulls were changing places with those who had been sleeping.

It could have been no more than a couple of hours later, judging by the position of the moon, that Maung Po gradually awoke with the feeling there was something wrong. He threw off the fold of Ma Hla's ear that covered him and sat up, waking her for a moment. She gave him a reassuring nudge. Still Maung Po felt uneasy, and looked around the clearing. The guardians were at their posts, but two of them were so motionless that he wondered if they could be asleep standing up.

He heard a suspicious rustle of leaves off to the right of the clearing. The sentry nearest the noise didn't stir, and Maung Po was sure now that the animal must be asleep.

38

He looked over at the great mound that was U Tun and wondered what he should do.

Surely the other guardians would sense it if there were danger! And who was he, Maung Po, third son of the Thugyi, to know more than the guardians? For everyone knows that even if elephants don't see well, they have the best hearing and the greatest wisdom of all animals.

Just then Maung Po heard a clink of metal from the same direction. Instantly he got to his hands and knees and crawled around the sleeping forms to U Tun's side. He paused, thinking that if U Tun should wake with a start, he might well be crushed, so close were the elephants lying.

He barely touched U Tun's shoulder in order not to startle him, and immediately U Tun took a sniff of Maung Po and then raised his trunk, feeling the air. Up came the great head, the ears quivering in their effort to listen.

Click! came another noise. Maung Po was sure of it this time. U Tun got up without a sound and quietly picked his way among the sleepers and crossed the clearing to the side of one of the drowsy guardians. Maung Po followed to the edge of the ring of sleepers and watched as U Tun, using his trunk, nudged the offender on the ear. The guardian started, then immediately began trying to sense danger.

U Tun turned back to the herd just as Maung Po heard another noise on the opposite side of the clearing. The sentinel on the nearer side was alert, though, and he froze in an attitude of listening. U Tun heard it too—as must some of the others, for Maung Po noticed several of them rising. Ma Hla was already up, and Maung Po was about to return to her when he was swung up to the shoulders of an elephant with tusks so long that he knew it could only be U Tun.

He kicked behind the right ear to head U Tun toward Ma Hla, with whom he felt more at home, but there was no response. U Tun, as did the others, stood tensely waiting to see what threatened. Even the baby elephants, Maung Po noticed, knew that something was wrong—they stood close by their mothers, alert.

U Tun took a step toward the trail and then froze at another noise, this time on a third side of the clearing. Head raised full, trunk extended—almost to the treetops, it seemed to Maung Po—tail ramrod-stiff and quivering with anticipation of action, U Tun was indeed a leader.

Maung Po was no longer afraid of U Tun; he felt proud to be borne by him. And he felt something else—and this for the first time: the feeling of being at one with another. Maung Po knew that he loved Ma Hla, but for U Tun he felt something different. U Tun was a warrior, thugyi of the large herd, and because Maung Po had warned him of danger, U Tun knew him as one of his own and took him on his shoulders. Now U Tun and Maung Po were one. And that is as Maung Po would have wanted it to be.

He sat U Tun very straight, his body tensed and his head slightly bent as he listened. There was a slight shuffling noise from behind; then they were joined by a bull elephant. Together the three listened.

Maung Po had not noticed this new arrival before. He wasn't quite as big as U Tun, nor were his tusks as long. Also, Maung Po had a feeling he was younger. Standing there, poised, waiting for the unknown danger, Maung Po thought that, even though he was smaller and younger, this bull still had a very able look about him. Ko Sein he would call him, after his father's assistant.

It was then that Maung Po saw the great scar across Ko Sein's chest. It was caked with mud, and Maung Po knew that Ko Sein must have covered it thus to help it heal—as he had heard elephants are likely to do. He wondered how the elephant had been wounded, and then thought that perhaps the scar might be a harness sore. For he remembered seeing an elephant train once, on their way to work in the teak forests, from where the elephants haul logs to be floated down-river to the saw. He heard again the clink of the trace chains dangling from heavy breast straps as they swung against the elephants' forelegs while the train shuffled along. He wondered if Ko Sein had been a work elephant who had turned wild and come back to the herd. Looking closer in the moonlight, Maung Po saw that Ko Sein's tusks had been blunted, and he was certain he was right.

A whispered command, very close, came to them. Immediately U Tun trumpeted loudly and headed straight for the trail. A riot broke out in the tense herd—the great lumbering bodies rushed after him with incredible speed.

As Maung Po on U Tun reached the trail, he saw two figures running down it toward them, carrying what looked like coils of heavy rope. Maung Po thought they must be surrounded by elephant-hunters, after the escaped Ko Sein.

The pair, seeing the herd upon them, stopped in fear. Ko Sein, when he scented them, almost threw Maung Po off U Tun as he rushed past in full charge, trunk coiled tightly between his tusks, and head lowered, ready.

In the face of this charge, one of the men leaped from the trail into the thick brush, as the other turned to run but became tangled in his rope and fell with a loud cry. In almost the same instant Ko Sein was on him and, with his tusks, as a man with a fork might flip a strip of bacon from a plate, scooped him up and sent him hurtling through the air, to land, broken, on a high tree limb, from which he dangled as the herd went roaring down the trail beneath him.

Behind them Maung Po heard the sharp crack of what he knew must be rifle fire. It sounded quite different from his father's shotgun—not as big a noise but somehow more powerful. His father's gun was the only gun in the valley, and the village was very proud that their thugyi alone, among all the thugyis of the valley, should be permitted a shotgun. It was a mark of trust and respect for the village.

More and more rifles were added to the firing behind

them, and Maung Po thought it strange that elephant-hunters bent on capture of a renegade should be doing so much shooting. Then, at a bend in the trail where the moonlight was brighter, he had his answer. Some soldiers wearing helmets were trying to set up a strange gun on three legs, and he knew that these must be the enemy. They must be trying to capture elephants to haul their supplies, Maung Po decided, and he thought that no matter how strong and cruel the enemy were, they certainly didn't know much about elephants.

That was the last of the soldiers with the gun on three legs. Ko Sein didn't even bother to charge this time, but just kept going in his headlong rush, without changing stride, right through them, followed by the herd. Whatever lay in the elephants' path was ground into the earth.

The firing grew fainter and finally stopped. Maung Po wondered how many of the elephants had been hit. When they reached a fork in the trail the winded herd came to a halt, and Maung Po had a chance to look them over.

While he couldn't tell whether any were missing, it was still a very large herd. He thought that if any were lost some of the herd would be looking back down the trail. But the only ones interested in what lay behind were two bulls who were standing guard, ready to warn the rest of pursuit. Maung Po, smiling, imagined it would take the enemy a while to sort themselves out.

The herd milled about for a while as though trying to make up their minds which fork to choose. Finally, U Tun chose the trail to the east, while Ko Sein set out on the more southerly one. The herd divided themselves more or less evenly between the two leaders, but Maung Po noticed that U Tun seemed to have more mother elephants and calves in his train.

As U Tun's group set off, Maung Po, atop the broad head, settled down for what he knew would be a long trek. Directly behind them followed Ma Hla, and it gave Maung Po a warm feeling to have her so close. Ahead were two warrior elephants acting as advance guard, while the herd, following, took up U Tun's fast pace. Each mother guided her calf by resting her trunk along its side.

45

If the calf strayed or slowed up, the trunk was there, ready with a scolding.

Maung Po didn't know where they were going but he was sure U Tun did. And he didn't know whether it would be a good place or a bad place. All he knew was that he had faced the enemy and their fire and that he was happy in the company of the herd. Wherever they went or whatever they did, for Maung Po it would be all right if U Tun were there.

Four

They trekked East for three days, resting during the
daylight hours and moving at night. The jungle growth
began thinning on the second day, and Maung Po realized that they had reached a part of Burma very different
from any he had known. It was hill country, and as they
entered a dry, almost desert-like valley on the last day of

47

the trek Maung Po could see a distant range of mountains.

The herd hung back in the jungle at the edge of the valley during the day and waited until night to cross it. Maung Po decided this must be because there was little cover in the valley and the elephants could be seen so easily by the enemy.

He wondered if they would find water in the valley— for, looking at the herd, he saw how badly they needed water, forage, and rest. The mountains looked very high, and he hoped that the herd would have the strength to cross them. And he wondered about the group led by Ko Sein—where they were and whether they would ever rejoin the main herd.

This was not Maung Po's idea of war. For here were no glorious battles. Here Maung Po saw only long marches at night without enough food or water, hiding from the enemy. War, Maung Po decided, is not a good thing—it is more hiding than fighting.

When darkness fell, the herd started across the valley, but this time with six or eight of the younger bulls spread out ahead as advance guard. The herd itself soon began to wander, and the pair of bulls who made up the rear guard had a hard time keeping their charges together. Using their trunks as a means of persuasion, they would urge the stragglers on, and when this didn't work, the bulls took to butting them. Several times this resulted in fights among the herd, and then U Tun would have to go to the rear to straighten things out.

48

They reached the foothills by dawn—and just in time, too, for far down the valley in the moonlight Maung Po made out a column of soldiers on the march. He didn't bother to warn U Tun because the soldiers were so far away; he knew that by the time they met the elephants' tracks, the herd would be safe in the cover of the foothills.

Maung Po was surprised that they were still in country occupied by the enemy. Surely, he thought, the enemy must be everywhere; and he wondered about his village—whether by this time the enemy had reached it, and if he should have remained there to help defend it. For with the enemy at the gates, everyone would fight—even he, Maung Po, third son of the Thugyi.

Out of some faint memory U Tun picked up an old and long unused trail leading into the hills. Once on the trail he set such a pace that the advance guard was hard put to it to keep ahead of him. Maung Po hoped that U Tun knew where he was leading them, for the trail seemed to twist and turn more and more, the farther they went along it. Then, as they topped a ridge, Maung Po knew everything would be all right, for there below them in the half-light he saw something that shone—water! It was a spring bordered by lush grasses and stands of bamboo. Maung Po was glad in his heart, for here the herd might be saved. He laughed and, leaning forward, kissed the top of U Tun's head in his joy that U Tun had led them so true.

Well watered, the herd turned to the rich grass and the

juicy bamboo with all the hunger of their three-day trek. Maung Po discovered a mango tree—an important discovery, for bamboo shoots and mangoes were favorite delicacies. Ma Hla hung close by him, however, and a couple of times even made offerings with her trunk, but these Maung Po politely refused. There was a certain satisfaction in being on his own again that he enjoyed.

When his appetite was finally satisfied, Maung Po took a stroll back down the trail to have a look around. Two guardians well back scented or heard him even before he saw them in the dim light, but recognizing him as one of them, turned their attention back to watchfulness for the enemy. Maung Po liked the feeling of their accepting him and not worrying about his presence.

He heard a noise behind him and upon turning, saw Ma Hla. She stopped some distance from him and listened, as if to see what he was up to. A little annoyed by this concern, Maung Po went up to her, wondering how to tell her he was quite capable of looking after himself, but she offered her trunk so nicely that he thought it would be rude not to accept. So he let her carry him back to the spring, where he found the herd standing quietly, to sleep out the day.

As he settled down on Ma Hla's broad head Maung Po was smiling. Closing his eyes, he wondered lazily about Ko Sein and where his group could be. And he wondered about himself and his luck in finding such good friends as Ma Hla and U Tun. This was not the way he had intended to fight the war, of course, but right now, sleepy and well fed, he couldn't think of a better way.

Refreshed, the herd set out on the trail again that night. This trail climbed all the way, and in some places became so steep that the herd had to watch their footing. It became cooler as the night wore on, and finally Maung Po got off U Tun and walked to keep himself warm. U Tun kept in touch with him by resting his trunk on Maung Po's shoulder as a guide, to avoid stepping on him in the darkness. It was like a father's hand resting there, if a rather heavy one. Each time Maung Po shrugged it off, back it would come, with a little puff of breath by way of rebuke. Finally Maung Po gave in and accepted his burden, and before long he was glad he had.

There was a sudden hiss in front of him and even as he heard it Maung Po felt himself swung high in the air to safety. The action was so quick, it was over almost before he knew it. Maung Po knew a cobra must have been there ready to strike and that U Tun with his great foot had ground the snake into the earth while he swung Maung Po clear. How did U Tun know it was there? the boy wondered. He was sure U Tun couldn't have seen it, and he was sure U Tun could not have been warned by the hiss, for there wasn't enough time. Maybe U Tun had sensed danger, but however he had known that the cobra was there, Maung Po was glad he had.

Looking ahead, Maung Po thought he could make out some large shapes standing in a place where the trail seemed to be joined by another. As they drew closer he saw that the shapes were elephants and that there were too many to be the advance guard. Could it be? . . . he wondered.

Then he knew he was right. It was Ko Sein, with his part of the herd waiting there quietly for them! What a snuffling and trunk-weaving now took place! Old friends, fellow warriors, even lovers, were reunited! The babies gamboled about, bumping into one another; the elders with dignity rocked in a rhythmic dance of greeting; and some of the warriors playfully tried make-believe charges against one another that Maung Po was careful to stay well out of the way of. And watching it all, but standing apart from it, were U Tun and Ko Sein, kings in their own right—wise, fearless, true.

At dawn the herd, now all together, resumed their trek, with U Tun taking the lead and Ko Sein the rear. Maung Po supposed this was so that if the enemy attacked both ends of the column would have leadership.

He noticed that U Tun had increased the pace and wondered if this meant they were in safe country and U Tun wanted to get the trek over with. But then, the advance guard still worked the trail ahead with great caution, so Maung Po realized it wasn't due to a feeling of increased safety.

It was after several hours' march, when the weaker ones began to fail, stringing the column well out—much to the annoyance of Ko Sein—that Maung Po saw the

advance guard come to a sudden halt, trunks up, scenting danger. The column pulled up short and in a moment all that could be heard was the heavy breathing of the great, tired bodies.

U Tun kept shifting his weight out of nervousness, and Maung Po knew that here must be something the elephant didn't like. He slid down from U Tun and then crept quietly along the trail to have a look for himself. The advance guard let him pass, and, seeing a break in the trail ahead where it was flooded in morning light, Maung Po dropped on all fours and crawled.

What he saw from his lying position as he looked down a steep bank filled him with fear. For there below was a deep *chaung,* or dry river bed, its sides like those of a canyon. Directly ahead where the trail eased down a slope to the chaung edge was a wooden bridge with a dirt road leading to it.

Then Maung Po heard the sound of motors, and soon three enemy trucks loaded with supplies came along the road on his side of the chaung, raising great clouds of dust. They turned onto the bridge and rumbled across it with surprising speed. Maung Po looked at the bridge and thought that perhaps the enemy didn't know much about trapping elephants, but there was no doubt that they could build fine bridges.

He turned back toward the advance guard. They were nervous and looked as if they might break and run. Maung Po knew how sensitive elephants' hearing is, and how much the rumble of the trucks crossing the bridge must have worried them.

Taking another look at the bridge, Maung Po saw now what U Tun's plan must have been. For across the chaung, as far as the eye could reach, he saw level plains heavy with grass waving in the breeze. He knew that the occasional groves of trees he could see would make ideal cover both from the sun and from the enemy. By the look of it there was water in that country, and by the look of it he knew this must be the promised land of the herd.

That long, hard trek to this beautiful land only to find it occupied by the enemy! Quietly Maung Po began to weep.

Five

Maung Po didn't know what U Tun would do now, but he did know that the enemy must have built their bridge right on the old elephant trail. Probably it was the only place along the whole length of the chaung that they could bridge. And he knew this must be the only place the herd could cross, too, because as far as he had been able to see, up and down the chaung there were steep cliffs.

He returned to the uneasy herd as another convoy of trucks rumbled over the bridge, certain that whatever U Tun decided to do, he would do nothing until darkness fell.

The herd waited the day out patiently. U Tun never moved from where he had stopped, and the advance guard never gave up their watchfulness. Several times Maung Po walked the length of the column of elephants and each time wondered at their complete silence and patience. They were not sleeping, but simply standing immobile, waiting till their time should come.

The day went quietly too. A few more convoys passed by in the morning, and in the afternoon these and others returned. Maung Po could tell by the sound that the returning convoys were running empty. Idly he wondered what the enemy on the other side of the chaung would do if they had no supplies. What would they do for bullets for their guns? What would they do for food for their bellies? He heard the rumbling in his own belly and remembered how hungry he was. He knew that, thanks to what Ma Hla had taught him about the right leaves, herbs, and grasses, he could feed himself. But he wondered how long the enemy's bellies could hold out without supply trucks to bring their food to them.

As soon as it was dark U Tun headed quietly for the bridge. The herd made as if to follow, but a grunt from U Tun stopped them. He passed the advance guard and, nearing the edge of the bank at the end of the trail, he stopped and spent a long time sniffing the air for danger.

Satisfied that all was well, he worked his way down the bank and went toward the bridge, followed at some distance by Maung Po, who kept to the shadows cast by a faint moon.

When he reached the ramp leading up to the bridge U Tun stopped and listened for what seemed to Maung Po an endless time. He snuffled at the ground with the greatest care, as if suspecting a trap. He even inspected the shoulders at each side of the bridgehead where the precipices fell away less sharply, trying each one to see if it could be climbed.

But his real interest was in the bridge itself. He spent a long time snuffling at the side rails and the timbers of the floor. Finally he tested it with one forefoot and then the other. Satisfied at last, he stepped onto it, bringing his full weight to bear. Then he slowly made his way across it to the other side, the bridge making barely a creak, so cautiously did he step.

Maung Po crossed the bridge behind U Tun and waited for him to complete his inspection. Then he tapped the elephant on the shoulder and U Tun swung him up, giving as he did so a low, whistle-like sound. At this signal, one by one and well spaced out, the herd came down the bank from the trail and silently crossed the bridge. When they reached the far side they formed a protective circle, with a few guardians standing alert out in the plains.

Maung Po watched with admiration as they crossed the bridge in silence, and he compared this to the great rumble the enemy trucks made. He wondered again what would happen if no supply trucks crossed the chaung. Suddenly he had an idea—an idea so strong he almost fell off U Tun. It might work, he thought. And he was certain the elephants could do it if he, Maung Po, once got U Tun started.

Gingerly he kicked with his right heel to turn U Tun toward the shoulder beside the ramp to the bridge. U Tun stiffened in surprise. Maung Po kicked harder, and up came the trunk, as if U Tun was about to pluck him off like a fly.

Desperately Maung Po gave three of the hardest kicks he could. He felt U Tun relax, then turn toward the shoulder. Maung Po wanted to hug him, he was so happy. But he knew that his arms would barely go round the giant's trunk, let alone his neck.

At the precipice U Tun halted uncertainly, but Maung Po urged him down with pressure from both heels. He knew that some of the herd would follow, if he could only get U Tun down to the chaung bed.

After much careful picking of his way, U Tun made it. A rattle of stones behind them told Maung Po that others were following. He turned U Tun toward one of the up-right logs supporting the bridge, which he could see outlined darkly against the white gravel of the chaung bottom.

Puzzled, U Tun took his time. Maung Po had the feeling that U Tun didn't like any of it; and he also had the feeling that if U Tun didn't rebel it would be only because of his trust in him—Maung Po, third son of the Thugyi.

U Tun stood before the upright and balked. Maung Po urged him even harder, and finally U Tun pressed his broad head against it. There was a sharp crack and then a groan from the timber, and Maung Po knew that his idea would work.

Several bulls crowded round out of curiosity as Maung Po again urged U Tun forward. This time U Tun leaned into the upright with all his weight. Maung Po could feel him straining and heard his feet trying to get a hold in the loose gravel.

Getting the idea, some of the bulls began trying other uprights, but did not make much progress. Then Maung Po thought of something. As he urged U Tun forward again he called out, "Hoom!" Then he repeated it as U Tun eased up, and kept calling it out slowly and steadily as the elephants worked, until a regular rhythm was established.

From the groans it was making Maung Po knew that the bridge must be swinging back and forth like a man weaving about on stilts. At the end of one long push there was a crashing of timbers, and the bridge fell. And it fell as Maung Po hoped it would—away from them.

The elephant next to U Tun raised its trunk in a great

trumpeting salute. Laughing, Maung Po turned toward it to share his pleasure in their victory with this bull, and found to his surprise that it was no bull but Ma Hla, who had been straining away with the best of them!

The herd climbed the bank with much rattling of stones, and Maung Po hoped that the loose gravel of the chaung would disguise the prints of the elephants' feet so the enemy would think that the bridge fell of its own accord. By the time U Tun had headed the herd toward a banyan grove across the plain, light was coming up in the east.

Maung Po looked back at the chaung. There was what had once been a bridge. There was a bridge destroyed— Maung Po's brothers and their whole army couldn't have done better! There was a present from Maung Po to the enemy!

After drinking from a water hole on the far side of the banyan grove, the herd spent the day under cover of the grove. Maung Po began watching Ko Sein with great interest. Of all the herd he was the only one that kept his distance from Maung Po, just as now he was the only one made nervous by remaining close to the bridge, which meant man. Remembering the soldiers he had charged on the jungle trail, Maung Po thought how much Ko Sein must hate man. As Ko Sein looked at him it occurred to Maung Po that he had never seen an elephant before with cold eyes. Maung Po shivered and was glad that whoever had done hurt to Ko Sein, it hadn't been he.

Faintly, from far across the plain, Ko Sein caught the sound of trucks, and instinctively he set himself for the charge. The sound worried Maung Po too, and he climbed the highest banyan tree in the grove and from an upper limb had a good view across the plain. He saw a long line of trucks drawn up on each side of the chaung where the bridge had been, and a lot of soldiers were standing on the edge, looking down at what had been their bridge. They stood there a long time, just looking.

Maung Po wondered why they didn't do something— rebuild the old one or start a new one. He didn't particularly care, but they really didn't seem like much of an army, just standing there gazing at a bridge that was no more. He glanced down at the herd beneath him; they were resting quietly—except for Ko Sein. He was still weaving back and forth and taking vicious swipes at flies that bothered him.

Just below Maung Po's perch there was a comfortable-looking crotch in the tree, and into this he crawled and settled down for a nap. As he dropped off, he could hear a distant truck occasionally and Ko Sein snorting nervously.

When he woke up it was late afternoon. The herd was stirring, ready to leave the grove to graze on the plain. Maung Po didn't see Ko Sein among them, and, yawning lazily, he climbed to the upper limb for another look at the enemy. He had barely reached the top of the tree when he heard the sound of rifle fire coming from the chaung. Beneath him the troubled herd crowded into the center of the grove for better cover.

The firing increased until soon there was so much shooting that it sounded like a battle. Because of a cloud of dust rising from the chaung it was hard for Maung Po to see, but he thought he could make out what looked like an elephant pushing one of the trucks toward the precipice. Maung Po hadn't known the enemy were using elephants in their supply trains, and was wondering if they had many, when he noticed that the soldiers seemed to be shooting at the elephant.

Then it came to him—it was Ko Sein! He heard what he knew must be a gun that fired very fast and very long added to the firing, and still Ko Sein kept pushing the truck to the edge. He noticed now that quite a few soldiers were hanging over the open sides of the truck, strangely still. He wondered why they didn't jump, and then realized they must have been hit by the shots meant for Ko Sein.

Then in a great cloud of dust the truck, the soldiers, and Ko Sein, still pushing, disappeared over the edge. Ko Sein had done it!

The firing died out and Maung Po climbed slowly down the tree. He went to the edge of the grove and listened as darkness fell. Presently he heard the sound of the trucks going away.

Maung Po wondered about Ko Sein. He knew Ko Sein

had done a brave deed, and yet he couldn't help wondering if it were really worth it. A few enemy soldiers and a truck hardly seemed worth the life of such a brave elephant. Then too, Ko Sein had left the grove on his own and if he had been seen, soldiers might have come and the whole herd been endangered. Ko Sein couldn't be trusted, and Maung Po knew that if there were even one elephant U Tun couldn't trust in the herd, soon there would be no herd.

And Maung Po wondered once more what men had done to Ko Sein to make him hate them so. Remembering the soldiers still in the truck as it went over the edge of the precipice, he knew that Ko Sein had found the end he would have chosen.

A rising restlessness in the herd stopped Maung Po's speculations and he returned to them in the center of the grove. Even U Tun was uneasy, and Maung Po felt that the leader wanted to leave this country behind them. He acted as if he wouldn't mind leaving Maung Po behind too, for no amount of tapping on the great elephant's shoulder would get him to offer his trunk. Before long U Tun headed toward the edge of the grove, in the direction of the distant hills, and Maung Po knew that a new trek had begun.

As U Tun shuffled off, Ma Hla offered Maung Po her trunk, and he accepted gladly. She was really more comfortable than U Tun, anyway. Yes, he decided, settling himself more securely, he had missed Ma Hla.

Six

The herd spent the night on the march, and by daybreak reached even higher ground, which they found too cool. Still, there was ample water and grass—though of a kind Maung Po had never seen before—and fair cover. They saw no sign of the enemy.

Maung Po wondered that they never saw a village or sign of man, and was surprised to find Burma such a big country. He had always thought Burma was mostly his own village and the valley in which it lay, with Rangoon, the Jewel of Burma, and its great pagoda at the end of it. He saw now that there was a lot to Burma the people of his village didn't know about—even his father, the Thugyi. He supposed by this time his brothers, too, must have discovered how big a country Burma really is.

The herd was not happy in the highlands, and Maung Po knew that their stay would not be a long one. The nights were too cool for their comfort, and the new grass did not agree with them. Maung Po remembered the warm breezes of the plain, and its rich grasses, and he wondered if U Tun was having the same thoughts.

But Maung Po wasn't long in finding out, for in a few days U Tun set out for the plain—and with a pace the herd found hard to follow, even though it was largely downgrade and good going. There was one swamp to cross, but this they did at daybreak of the second day. They reached good cover on the far side of the swamp, from which they could see the plain below. And way across the plain, in the direction of the road to the chaung, a column of dust hung in the air, which meant to Maung Po that a new bridge was being built. Even so, it was a good sight, the plain.

That night they crossed the plain to the banyan grove, grazing as they went. At dawn Maung Po searched the grove carefully for signs of human footprints—he wanted to be sure that in their absence the enemy hadn't discovered their hideout. He found nothing. But the herd was restless as they waited out the day in the cover of the grove, and every now and then there was the sound of heavy guns firing in the distance—it wasn't so much noise as a pressure shaking the air. Maung Po knew the guns must be very heavy indeed, and that meant that the battle would be an important one.

He watched the cloud of dust hanging in the sky over the place where the bridge had been. Surely, he thought, the enemy must be very busy building their new bridge to raise so much dust. He decided to climb his tree for a better look, and while he couldn't see very much of the building of the new bridge through the dust, what he

saw along the road on the other side of the chaung leading to the bridge made him gasp. As far as he could see
there was a solid line of supply trucks and troops waiting
for the bridge to be finished so they could cross. He had
never known there were so many trucks in all the world,
let alone that the enemy would have so many. Soldiers,
yes—everyone knew there were lots of enemy soldiers.
But that long line of trucks which stretched for miles!
For a long time Maung Po looked at them in wonder as
he lay prone on the limb of the tree.

He knew that most of the trucks were used not for
carrying the soldiers of the enemy but for carrying all
the things they needed for fighting—bullets, food, gaso-
line for the tractors that pulled the big guns, bandages
for the enemy doctors to use, medals for the soldiers that
were brave, beautiful swords for the officers.

Maung Po marveled at the number of things the enemy
needed to make their soldiers soldiers. And he thought
of his brothers and the young men of his village going off
to war, some of them carrying only dahs, and smiled as
he realized that it didn't take much to make his people
into soldiers who could fight. And if the enemy didn't
have all these miles of things they needed, how well
would they fight?

Suddenly the thought came to Maung Po that perhaps
he and the herd had done a lot more than just knock
down an enemy bridge. He listened again to the sound
of the great guns in the distance and was more sure than

71

ever that the battle was an important one. And there lined up on the road across the chaung were all the things the enemy needed to win it! And only he, Maung Po, the child too young to go to war, knew why before long those big guns would be quiet and his people with their dahs would finally have a chance—unless, of course, the enemy finished their new bridge in time to feed the big guns. This thought did not make Maung Po very happy, and he wondered as he looked at the dust cloud how long it would take to finish the bridge.

He climbed down the tree and went over to Ma Hla and sat down next to her, using her forefoot for a backrest. She stirred lazily and gave a twitch of her trunk in welcome. Thinking still of the new bridge, Maung Po watched U Tun with great interest—clearly the elephant was still restless. He swayed back and forth unceasingly and kept sniffing the air in the direction of the distant guns. Several of the warrior bulls stood close by him, as if waiting for orders. Maung Po knew U Tun had something on his mind, and wondered if he might soon try to lead the herd to new grazing grounds well away from the sounds of battle.

Where would the herd go? he wondered. They certainly wouldn't work down the plain toward the battle, and they had already tried the highlands. That left only a return to the jungle they had come from, on the other side of the chaung—which meant trying to cross the chaung where the enemy was working on their new

bridge. Maung Po didn't think U Tun would be likely
to risk that, yet he knew if they remained very long near
the grove, the battle might come to them. Whatever the
herd would do, Maung Po knew he would have to wait
until night to find out. And he knew he should wait until
night for a look at the new bridge.

But Maung Po didn't wait for night. In the late afternoon he quietly slipped out of the grove and headed for
the bridge. He noticed Ma Hla watching anxiously from
the shadows at the edge of the grove, but he knew he
was safe from the eyes of the enemy in the long grass
that grew higher than his head. As he worked his way
along he began to hear the sound of lighter guns firing,
and he thought the battle must be moving nearer. That
must mean that the enemy were already feeling the need
of all their supplies waiting on the other side of the
chaung, and that if his people forced the enemy back to
the edge of the chaung, there could be no further retreat.

It looked to Maung Po as if he were finally going to
take part in a real battle. He smiled as he imagined he
might be able to find his brothers and stand shoulder to
shoulder with them in the thick of it. If only he hadn't
lost his dah that night he left his village! For, armed with
his dah, small though it might be, who then would dare
to laugh and say he was too young to fight as he slashed
the enemy right and left, along with his brothers? There
would be a fine thing, and on his return home from the
war the people of his village would hear of it, and he

might be known then, not as third son of the Thugyi, but as son of the Thugyi!

He paused to rest hidden in the long grass and was thinking of the glorious part he might soon take in the battle when he noticed a distant light in the sky in the gathering dusk. What a great light the guns make, he thought, and then for the first time wondered what would happen to the herd if the battle should come to them. Would U Tun be able to prevent the elephants' stampeding in their terror at the great noise of the guns? And if they stampeded, blinded by the flashes of the guns, might not they rush right into the middle of it and be cut down like trees of the forest in the rivers' flood? Maung Po forgot all about the glories of battle suddenly, and thought only of Ma Hla, U Tun, the mothers with their young at their sides, and the beautiful warrior bulls, so proud in their strength.

Maung Po knew it would take more than their strength to save the herd if the battle should come to them. Worried, he started off once more toward the bridge, determined to have a look at it and to try to find a way to get the herd clear of the plain, which was no longer a haven of lush grasses, but a trap in which the herd might find themselves squeezed between two armies.

It was night, with a new moon, by the time Maung Po reached the chaung. From here—there being little cover—he crawled on his belly to a point from which he could get a good view of the work on the bridge. He could see that the enemy had built new piers to support it, and that they had taken no chances with its coming down easily this time. The timbers were much more massive than the old ones and in addition were supported by thick steel cables. With relief he realized that they would still have to build several more piers before they reached his side of the chaung and were able to lay their planking across it. By that time, he knew, the battle might well be won.

He stayed hidden long enough to be sure that the bridgehead was unguarded on his side and then crawled to the edge of the ramp and looked directly down into the chaung. He almost laughed out loud at the scene below him. For the enemy were in such a hurry to get the bridge finished that the swarm of soldiers at work were getting in one another's way. The chaung looked to Maung Po just like an anthill as the soldiers crawled over and under the timbers and ran back and forth, bumping into each other in the half-light.

Maung Po watched as a crowd of soldiers tried to lift a heavy timber on which stood three enemy officers arguing among themselves, while at the same time shouting orders to the soldiers. The soldiers finally raised the timber waist high, but then let it drop, spilling the officers. Raging, the officers got up and started beating the soldiers' backs with the flat of their swords. Maung Po admired the swords and thought how much he would like to have one, for he knew they were of fine steel and

that, broken off short, they would make excellent dahs.

It was as he was envying the enemy officers their swords that he noticed how the light shone from their blades. It seemed a very bright light to be coming from a new moon, and, looking over his shoulder, he saw that the whole plain was lit in a red glow. A great fire was sweeping through the grass toward the grove. Already it had passed the grove on its far side toward the highlands, thus cutting off the herd's escape in that direction. Maung Po was frightened by the speed with which the flames raced across the plain, turning night into day, and knew he must get back to the herd before it was too late.

He crawled as far as the long grass, hearing as he did so the firing from the battle sounding even closer. He got to his feet, ready to run toward the grove, when before him loomed the enormous shape of U Tun. Maung Po thought he had never looked bigger.

As U Tun passed him, heading for the chaung, Maung Po reached out to hold him back, but U Tun with a swing of his trunk pushed him out of the way. He was followed by half a dozen warriors, with Ma Hla bringing up the rear. She paused for a moment by Maung Po, then followed the warriors to the chaung edge. The rest of the herd hung back, silent in the long grass.

Maung Po heard shouts coming from the chaung and knew that U Tun and the warriors with Ma Hla must have been seen by the soldiers as they stood by the chaung edge, well lit by the fire. U Tun wheeled and, followed by the warriors, set off at a fast pace along the chaung. Almost before he knew it, Maung Po felt himself swung up to Ma Hla's .broad shoulders as she hurried after U Tun. Looking behind, Maung Po saw the rest of the herd in a near stampede trying to catch up with them, the young scampering full out after their mothers. And then across the plain pursued by the racing flames he could make out the running figures of men and heard voices shouting. It was the enemy, he was sure, and he knew that if his people didn't cut them down by the time they reached the bridgehead, the fire would.

Here was a tale to tell his father the Thugyi, his mother, and his sisters! But would they believe it? Would anybody believe the tales Maung Po would have to tell of war? He had never thought of that, and the possibility of never being believed saddened him. He thought instead of the shuffling stride of the herd—the shuffle that was neither trot nor gallop and yet could cover so much ground in a day. Over the roar of the fire and the sounds of the battle he could hear the sea of grass along the edge of the chaung whish as the herd passed through it, and the sound was soothing to him. It was, he knew, a sound he would miss when he returned to his village someday and told his tales of war.

Maung Po didn't know where U Tun was leading them, but he was certain that U Tun must have a purpose as he followed the course of the chaung. It didn't seem to matter to Maung Po where they were going as long as

U Tun led them. For he knew that wherever the bull elephant led, it would be for the safety of the herd. Maung Po trusted U Tun, and that was enough.

He lay flat along Ma Hla's head and remembered all she had done for him since he had left his village. A great warm tide of love flowed through him both for her and all the herd as they hurried through the grass, the elephants' rough hides turned red in the light of the fire. He felt more than just a boy playing soldier. He felt . . .

Well, Maung Po felt he might be very close to being a man. And he thought perhaps it wouldn't matter much if nobody believed his tales of war, for he might never tell anybody. In fact, he might never return to the village at all.

He looked up at the glow in the sky and smiled. Someday there would be no war in Burma, and that would be the time to worry about going home. Until then, there were U Tun, Ma Hla, the warriors . . .

Seven

Every now and then as U Tun led the herd along the
edge of the chaung in the flaming night he would pause
to test the steepness of the bank with a forefoot. At such
times the herd would mill about nervously, anxious to
get going again. But U Tun would not be hurried, and
Maung Po felt sure he must be trying to find some way
down into the chaung, and that there must be some
dimly remembered trail on its far side which might take
them to new and safer grazing grounds.

Each time U Tun decided that the place he had been
testing was not the right one, he would lead off again
at a fast pace as if to make up for lost time. They seemed
fairly to fly through the grass, and in the light of the fire,
Maung Po could see it close in again over their path so
that only a good tracker would be able to tell that an
elephant herd had passed by during the night. Of course,
it wouldn't matter now either to the enemy or to his own
people that an elephant herd was on the plain—they had
more important things to think about! But would either
ever believe, he wondered, that the outcome of the battle
would be due at least in part to him, Maung Po, third son

of the Thugyi, and U Tun and his herd? He didn't think
his brothers would ever admit such a possibility, even to
themselves.

Eventually U Tun found what he had been looking for
—one by one the elephants made their way carefully down
into the chaung at a place where the bank had been worn
into a path. Maung Po noticed that each waited its turn

patiently, however great was their desire to flee from the fire making its way across the plain toward them, and however frightened they were by the sounds of battle which drew steadily nearer. Three warrior bulls waited on guard out in the long grass until the others had gone safely down, and then took up the rear.

Once in the chaung, U Tun led them back in the direction of the bridge. Their progress was slow; the footing was bad, being mostly loose stone that must have been sharp, judging by the carefulness with which the elephants picked their way. Up ahead, Maung Po could see U Tun constantly turning toward the far bank, as if searching for something. He was sure now that he had been right in thinking there must be an old trail on the far side, and he wondered where it would come out.

Before long the herd stopped and waited, as U Tun turned to the bank and slowly started to climb up it. Watching him, Maung Po was amazed that an elephant could climb anything so steep, but, after almost falling twice, U Tun made it. Once on top, he had a good look around among the trees at the jungle edge, and then came back to the top of the chaung and raised his trunk triumphantly as a signal for the herd to follow.

When it was Ma Hla's turn, Maung Po found out how steep the bank really was—it was all he could do to keep from sliding down her back as she worked her way up the bank, sending down showers of stones to roll among those waiting below. One baby calf got halfway up, and

then, losing its footing, rolled, squealing, clear to the bottom. Its mother waiting on top gave a couple of scolding grunts, and this time the baby made it, aided by a good whack from a young bull to get it started.

When all the herd except the rear guard had made it up the bank, U Tun set off into the trees with such certainty that Maung Po felt sure he knew where he was going. Ma Hla hung back, however, and paid no heed to Maung Po's urgings. It was clear she didn't want to be at the head of the column with U Tun even if Maung Po, who didn't want to miss any excitement, thought differently. In fact, she seemed uneasy about following the herd at all, and Maung Po wondered if perhaps she had some special knowledge of danger ahead. Whatever it was, it didn't seem to Maung Po it could be any worse than the plain with its raging fire, which now had reached the other side of the chaung.

Finally Ma Hla started off after the herd, with only the rear guard behind. It made Maung Po angry to find himself at the end of the column and having to follow behind even the mothers with their young. But he didn't have much time to be angry because almost at once they were on a heavily overgrown trail that could not have been used in many years. The growth was so thick that it shut out the light from the fire and the sounds of battle—it was like a tunnel through the jungle, and it was so low that Maung Po had all he could do to hang on to Ma Hla. It seemed to take them forever to work out this trail, and as they neared its end, Maung Po was surprised to hear gunfire again and to see through the jungle growth the red glow in the sky.

The herd thrashed about in confusion in the undergrowth as Maung Po realized where they were. For he saw that this trail had led them back to the trail by which they had first come on their long trek to this part of the country, only to find the bridge at its end.

Then, as Ma Hla worked her way around the sides of the confused herd, Maung Po had a look at the trail end on the bank above the bridgehead. There below was a sight he would never forget! Across the chaung the whole plain seemed one great fire, and even in the flames Maung Po could see soldiers running and shooting. On their own side of the chaung he saw the endless line of waiting trucks and at the bridgehead itself great mountains of supplies piled up. Enemy soldiers were running back and forth, some shooting across the chaung and some even shooting at one another in the confusion. Officers waved their swords wildly and shouted orders that were never heard, while other soldiers dropped their rifles and ran along the chaung bed in search of safety. Suddenly there was a great explosion. A truck, which Maung Po knew must have been loaded with shells for the enemy's guns, blew up, and at that the herd stampeded down the slope and onto the old trail by which they had first come to the bridge.

Ma Hla held back, but the great rush of the herd down

to the trail caught her up in its flow, and down the slope she went with the others, Maung Po holding on for dear life. Just as she turned onto the old trail Maung Po saw an officer's sword lying by a great pile of boxes on the side of the trail. Without even thinking, he leaped down from Ma Hla's shoulders. His fall to the ground was so hard, it knocked his breath out. He was saved from being trampled by the rest of the herd only by lying still until he could get his breath. As each elephant rushed past him he wished over and over that he was still with Ma Hla.

When the last of the herd had gone crashing past he saw again through the dust the beautiful sword, and having got his breath back ran to the pile of boxes and picked it up. He gave it a great swing through the air, and even over the sound of battle he heard its blade sing. Now indeed Maung Po had a dah—or what would be a dah when he broke the blade off short—worthy of him! It would be the pride of his village, even as was his father the Thugyi's shotgun!

He held it up and turned it so that the light of the flames played on its highly polished blade. It was then that he saw Ma Hla hurrying back along the trail. He ran toward her proudly with his sword and just as she swung him up he saw an enemy soldier aiming one of those strange guns at her chest. It fired its many bullets very fast, and he felt Ma Hla shudder under him for an instant before she charged. The soldier went down, still firing, just as Ma Hla stumbled and almost fell.

Looking down, Maung Po saw that her forelegs were wet with blood. Knowing she must be badly hurt, he started to get down to help, but she turned back up the trail and hurried after the herd. Before she had gone very far they met U Tun and a warrior elephant who must have been waiting for them.

Ma Hla seemed determined to keep going and refused to stop for a rest even when U Tun and the warrior did. So they kept close to her, U Tun in the lead and the warrior behind. And so they carried on all day on the jungle track, with Maung Po still on Ma Hla, his sword cradled on his knees. They saw no sign of the herd, which Maung Po knew must be ahead.

Where were they going, he wondered, and why was Ma Hla in such a hurry to get there? He marveled at her strength—even so badly wounded she still kept on running—and he felt a great rush of love for her. He looked at his sword and suddenly hated it. He knew if he hadn't held Ma Hla up so long by taking it she wouldn't be wounded now.

He wondered if, supposing he threw the sword away, it might somehow make everything all right again. He thought about this for quite a while and finally decided it couldn't make any difference now—the harm was done. Besides, it *was* such a beautiful sword.

Gradually Maung Po began to feel there was something familiar about this part of the trail. Then Ma Hla turned from the trail and staggered through a curtain of vines, and at once Maung Po knew where they were, and why Ma Hla had had to come all this way.

They were at the Lost Pagoda, the elephants' dying place. As she reached the ruins she began to sway in a sad dance of farewell, then slowly sank to her knees and down. She settled gently, so as not to hurt him, her life ebbing away.

He kneeled by her head and looked in the sad eyes and at the softness in them that he loved so. Then she gave one great shaking breath and a film came across her eyes, covering the softness.

Maung Po felt the tears running down his cheeks, dropping to the sword that lay across his knees. He looked up, and all around them was the herd, standing silent.

After a long, last look at Ma Hla he drove the sword into the ground near her and left it there by her. He went over to U Tun and after a while the great warrior elephant offered his trunk and swung Maung Po up, as the herd stood by waiting. Slowly U Tun led off back to the trail that Maung Po knew would lead them to the valley in which his village lay. He looked back through the jungle growth at the Lost Pagoda. Ma Hla had finally come home; and Maung Po knew that before long he would be home too.

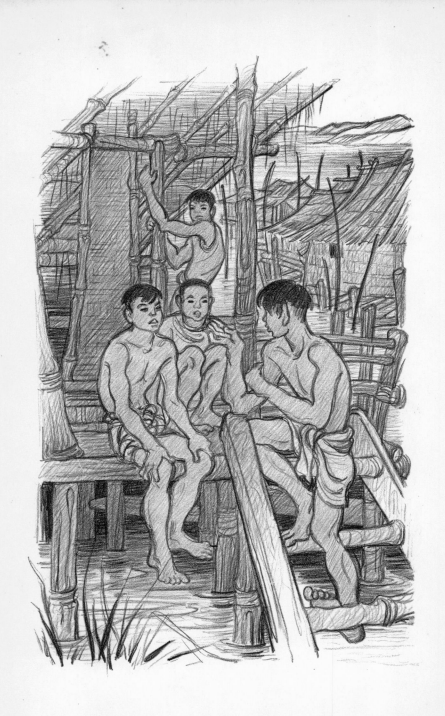

Well, the war is over in Burma and the people are free again. It is the rainy season there now, and the people of Maung Po's village have time to rest in their bashas, marvel at the great quantities of water the skies let down on them, and think of next year's rice crop.

And they may talk of the war and how glad they are that it is finished. And they may remember a tale of a bridge that the enemy built in a faraway place, and how a herd of wild elephants destroyed it and so a battle was won for their country. Or they may talk of a place deep in the jungle, that has never been found, where elephants go to die, and say that if one knew the place one could find there enough ivory to own all the rice paddies in Burma.

Or they may go in the rain to the Thugyi's basha to pass the time of day with him, and to question Maung Po, his third son. "Where were you, Maung Po, in that time of war?" they may ask. "Where did you go and what did you see?"

But Maung Po will only smile and say Burma is a great country of many wonders. And his brothers will answer, "But what can you know of this, Maung Po, a child, and our youngest brother?"

93

And Maung Po will think of one he loved, and remember the soft eyes and the things he felt in them. And he will say again, "Yes, Burma is a great country of many wonders." His father, the Thugyi, will smile and perhaps may take pride in the secret of his third son.

And somewhere in the jungle near the village gate a bull elephant may trumpet, calling to Maung Po, but he does not answer and only smiles at his father, his brothers, and the people of his village. And the people laugh at Maung Po for a child with his riddles, and go back to their bashas in the rain, shaking their heads and saying his name. Maung Po, they say—there is a good boy, even so.